TOMMY DONBAVAND'S FUNNY SHORTS

THERE'S A TIME PORTAL IN MY PANTS!

WRITTEN BY TOMMY DONBAVAND
ILLUSTRATED BY ALICE RISI

EDGE
FRANKLIN WATTS

LONDON • SYDNEY

Franklin Watts
First published in Great Britain in 2018 by The Watts Publishing Group

Credits
Executive Editor: Adrian Cole
Design Manager: Peter Scoulding
Cover Designer: Cathryn Gilbert
Illustrations: Alice Risi

HB ISBN 978 1 4451 5388 9
PB ISBN 978 1 4451 5390 2
Library ebook ISBN 978 1 4451 5389 6

Printed in China

Franklin Watts
An imprint of
Hachette Children's Group
Part of The Watts Publishing Group
Carmelite House
50 Victoria Embankment
London EC4Y 0DZ

An Hachette UK Company
www.hachette.co.uk

www.franklinwatts.co.uk

Contents

CHAPTER ONE
TEACHER

Jamal Jones stood at the front of the classroom and held out a cardboard shoe box. "This," he announced proudly, "is the Hamster Transportation Unit — Mark One!"

As the other pupils clapped loudly, Sarah Smith chuckled to herself. Jamal's invention for the upcoming science show was just so, well ... just so Jamal! He was nuts about animals, and he never missed a chance to include them in whatever he was doing.

"What a fantastic idea!" said Mr Pertwee.
He examined the outside of the box, onto
which Jamal had drawn pictures of his
numerous pets. There were fish, dogs, cats,
and even a snake or two. "So tell us, Jamal.
How does it work?"

Mr Pertwee had only arrived at the school a few weeks earlier, but he'd already made a big impact on the place. He always wore smart, stiff suits, had a big wave of red hair, and carried a beaming smile on his face everywhere he went.

Of course, everyone missed Mr Patrick and the different ways he had of making all the class laugh, but there was just something about Mr Pertwee. He made lessons come alive, especially his favourite subject — science. Just last month he'd announced the date of this year's Sladen School Science Show. Since then, everybody had been inventing and making all manner of weird and wonderful gadgets.

Already that morning, Alice had shown off her idea for Battery Operated Sprouts. Dan had demonstrated something he called Waterproof Soap and Claire had sprinkled the carpet in Ultra-Strong Dragon Repellent Powder. Mr Pertwee said that it must work perfectly as he hadn't seen a single dragon in the area for ages.

Next, it would be Sarah's turn to show off her creation. She clutched the small sewing kit in front of her, and glanced over at The Big Boffin — the award that would be given out for the most exciting science invention at the show. It was essentially a human brain (fake, of course), sprayed with gold paint and mounted on top of a short stand. Jamal called it the 'brain on a stick'.

Sarah desperately wanted it to be her name that was eventually engraved on the front. Then, she could introduce herself as Sarah Smith — scientist!

She turned her attention back to Jamal as he removed the lid of his creation.

"The Hamster Transportation Unit is cool! It's the perfect way to carry a hamster from point A to point B in comfort and style," said Jamal. "To some people, it might look like nothing more than an ordinary cardboard box, but you can see that I've taken a long time to decorate the sides, making it stand out as—"

He froze, a look of horror on his face. "Oh no!" he gasped.

"What's wrong?" asked Mr Pertwee.

"It's Franklin, my hamster!" cried Jamal.

"He's not in the transportation unit!"

"He's not?"

"No!" said Jamal, dropping to the floor.

"He's escaped!"

Screams erupted around the classroom as half the class tried to catch the runaway rodent, and the other half lifted their feet up onto their chairs.

"There's no need to panic!" Mr Pertwee assured everyone. "We don't want to upset Miss Howkins again!"

It took almost ten minutes — and a complaint from Miss Howkins in the class next door about the level of noise — to settle everyone back down. Although the pupils kept a sharp eye on the area around their desk, just in case Franklin appeared.

"OK, Sarah," said Mr Pertwee at last. "You're up ..."

Taking a deep breath, Sarah got to her

feet and walked the short distance to the front of the class. There, she turned to face her friends, and held up the small sewing kit. Reaching inside, she pulled out a sewing needle.

"Oooh," said Mr Pertwee. "I can already tell this is going to be good! It looks as though Sarah has discovered a new use for an ordinary, everyday item. Is that right?"

Sarah nodded, trying not to let her nerves show too much. She cleared her throat, and gave the short speech that she had been practising over and over in front of her wardrobe mirror for the past few days.

"For my entry to the Sladen School Science Show ..." she said.

Everyone in the class fell silent,
eager to hear what was coming next.
"I have invented time travel."

CHAPTER TWO
TIME

For once, Mr Pertwee was speechless.
His mouth opened and closed silently,
reminding Sarah of Jamal's collection
of tropical fish.

Eventually he said, "You've done what?"

"I've invented time travel, sir," said
Sarah. "Do you want to see how it works?"

"More than anything!" replied
Mr Pertwee.

"OK," said Sarah. "You've probably all

heard that time travel is impossible, right?"

The rest of the class nodded.

"Well, I think that's just because no-one has been able to find a way to work with the fabric of space and time," Sarah continued.

"Fabric?" said Jamal.

Mr Pertwee nodded. "That's what scientists call the relationship between time and space," he explained. "The two are linked together in a way that can't be separated."

"That's probably why my method allows you to travel to another place, as well as another time," said Sarah. "I'll show you ..."

Everyone in the room watched closely

as Sarah squinted at an empty space in the air right in front of her, as if searching for something almost invisible to the human eye. Then, she plunged her sewing needle into what appeared to be ... nothing.

Working quickly, she made stitching movements, weaving the needle away from her and back again — gradually marking out the shape of a circular doorway in the air.

Suddenly, Dan shouted out from his desk on the front row. "I can see something!"

"You can?" said Mr Pertwee, peering at the area around Sarah's hand. "Let me see." He hurried to kneel beside Patrick, and looked back at the area where Sarah was sewing.

"Oh my goodness!" he breathed.

There, in front of the entire class, a kind of doorway was beginning to form in the air. A doorway through which Class 4 could see into somewhere else. And somewhen else.

The place beyond Sarah's door looked like a library. Dark wooden shelves lined the

walls, each straining under the weight of hard-backed books with brown or red spines.

In the centre of the room sat a dark-coloured desk, padded with green leather. A chair in the same style sat just behind it. On the desk were several rolls of yellowing parchment paper, and a long, feathered quill pen jutted up from a brass pot of ink.

The room was lit by flickering candles that caused shadows to dance around the walls.

"I c-c-c-can't believe it!" stammered Mr Pertwee as Sarah finished. "That's the past!"

Sarah nodded as her fellow pupils gathered around the teacher in a mixture

of amazement and shock. She snapped
her length of invisible thread and
carefully dropped the sewing needle
back into its pouch.

Mr Pertwee's cheeks had turned white.
"Can I go through it?"

"Oh, yes," said Sarah. "Just be careful
that you don't break the portal I've sewn,
or you might not be able to get back."

"Portal?" said Jamal.

"This," said Sarah, gesturing to her handiwork, "is what I call a time portal."

"And I'm actually going to use it," said Mr Pertwee, his voice trembling. "Everyone else stay exactly where you are."

The class watched as their teacher tentatively approached the magical doorway. Taking care not to catch the edges with his jacket, he took a deep breath, then stepped through into another place and time.

The inside of the portal rippled as he crossed from one side to the other, like the surface of a pond after you've tossed in a pebble.

Mr Pertwee walked to the desk, and picked up one of the lengths of parchment. He unrolled it and held it up. A smile began to creep slowly across his face.

Just then, there was a noise from outside the room. Someone was coming!

Mr Pertwee quickly replaced the parchment and hurried back through the time portal — back to the present day.

The door to the library opened and a well-dressed man stepped through. He stopped and stared at Class 4 through the time portal.

"What on Earth?"

Quickly, Sarah reached up and broke the stitches at the top of the portal.

Instantly, the doorway to the past vanished.

"1755," announced Mr Pertwee. "It was 1755, and I was in Samuel Johnson's library, looking at an early draft of the first-ever dictionary! Sarah's invention works!"

The class erupted in cheers, not caring what the class next door thought about the noise.

Grinning, Sarah stuffed her sewing kit back into her pocket. Then she pulled it out again, realising she'd ripped a large hole in the pocket material.

"I must remember to repair that," she said to herself as she switched the sewing kit to her other pocket. "I don't want to lose my time needle."

CHAPTER THREE
TURKEY

The day of the Sladen School Science Show had finally arrived. Sarah finished brushing her hair and pulled on a freshly ironed shirt. She wanted to look her very best. She had even asked her dad to repair the hole in her trouser pocket the night before.

Sarah buttoned her waistcoat, and reached for the sewing kit on her bedside table. And that's when she realised that it was open.

Her heart pounded as she lifted the flap and peered inside the pouch.

Her time needle was missing.

"Dad!" she cried, racing down the stairs. "Where's my needle?"

"Needle?" said Dad, changing a nappy on Sarah's baby brother, Mikey. "Which needle?"

"The one that was in the sewing kit beside my bed!" said Sarah.

"Oh, that one," said Dad. "I borrowed it last night to fix that hole in your pocket."

"Thanks," said Sarah. "But where did you put the needle?"

"It's stuck in the reel of thread," her dad replied, pointing at the shelf.

"Phew! Got it," said Sarah with a sense of relief.

Mr Pertwee got to school early that morning. He wanted to set up all of the video cameras in the classroom to record the historic moment — proof that a real time portal could be created. As the pupils settled in their chairs, he stood at the front of the classroom, hardly able to contain his excitement.

"Boys and girls," exclaimed Mr Pertwee. "Welcome to the Sladen School Science Show!"

The pupils of Class 4 cheered and applauded, then quickly got to work unpacking their inventions and setting them out for inspection.

All except for Jamal, who was on his hands and knees again, still searching for his missing hamster. He had a carrot in his hand, and was making kissy-kissy noises as he crawled beneath the desks.

"Are you sure he's still in the classroom?" asked Sarah. "He might have got out."

Jamal sat up, banging his head on the underside of a table.

THUD!

"OUCH! No," he said, rubbing his scalp. "Franklin knows not to go off without telling me first ..."

"How would he … No, never mind." Sarah left Jamal to his hamster hunt. She reached into her repaired pocket and pulled out her sewing kit.

"Oh, cool!" said Jamal, his face appearing over the edge of her desk.

"What?" asked Sarah. "Have you found Franklin?"

"Not yet," said Jamal. "I mean your new time portal."

Frowning, Sarah moved around the table to join Jamal. She stood beside her friend and stared, her mouth wide open.

She had pulled a brand new time portal out of her pocket, connected to the stitches her dad had made while repairing the hole. He must have accidentally pushed the needle through the fabric of space and time, as well as the fabric of her trousers! "There's a time portal in your pants,"

Jamal laughed. Sarah turned and scowled at him. "Or, in your trousers ..." he added quickly.

Sarah and Jamal peered through the portal, which led to a lush, green forest. The ground was covered in unusual plants and bushes, and the bark on the massive tree trunks looked rough and knobbly.

"Where is that?" asked Jamal.

Before Sarah could reply, the greenery closest to the portal began to rustle, and then a small head popped out. It looked like a lizard, but a lizard that had feathers growing out of its neck.

"And what is that?" demanded Jamal.

Suddenly, the creature leapt out of the

bushes, through the portal and straight into the classroom. It was about the size of a turkey, but when it opened its mouth and let out a rasping SCREECH!, it sounded very different indeed.

"I think it's a dinosaur," hissed Sarah.

"Cool!" said Jamal.

"No, it's not cool," said Mr Pertwee, hurrying over.

Jamal frowned. "Why not?"

Mr Pertwee took a deep breath, hardly believing what he was about to say.

"Because, that is a velociraptor!"

CHAPTER FOUR
TERROR

"Everyone stay exactly where you are and DO NOT PANIC!" ordered Mr Pertwee.

Class 4 immediately began running around and screaming.

Miss Howkins banged repeatedly on the wall from the classroom next door.

"Mr Pertwee! Keep the noise down in there!" But it was almost impossible to hear her muffled shouts over the sound of the petrified pupils.

The velociraptor was clearly scared by the sudden surge in noise and movement. It ran from pupil to pupil, screeching and flapping its small arms.

As Sarah watched, the creature opened its mouth wide, revealing several rows of razor sharp teeth, then it bit down on a chair leg.

There was a CLANG! as dino tooth met metal. The chair toppled over as the damaged leg gave way and snapped.

SCREECH!

Now, the terrified raptor began to bite anything it could find — schoolbags, workbooks, and even a shoe someone had lost in the stampede to get away from it. This must have felt or tasted more like its

usual prey, as the dino paused long enough
to tear the leather footwear to pieces
before returning to its riotous rampage.

Mr Pertwee dashed from student to
student, trying to calm their nerves. He
reassured them that everything was going
to be OK. Then, he spotted a pair of girls
running towards the classroom door.

"NO!" he shouted. "Don't open the door, Lizzy! We can't let it get out of this room."

Lizzy froze, still gripping the door handle. "I'm scared, sir!"

"We're all scared," said Mr Pertwee, gently. "But we need to stay calm and think of a way out of this."

"How, sir?" cried Sarah, reaching for her needle. "Should I close the time portal?"

"No!" said Mr Pertwee quickly. "We don't want to trap the velociraptor in this time period. We don't know when, or even if, you would be able to open a window back to the Cretaceous period."

"Cretaceous period?" questioned Jamal. "But, I thought veloss ... vilass ... veloose

... those raptor thingies were from Jurassic times? They were in that movie."

"That's just artistic licence," said Mr Pertwee, skipping to one side as the dangerous dinosaur dashed past chasing a tennis ball someone had accidentally kicked. "They look very different to the way they were portrayed on screen as well."

"Yeah," agreed Sarah. "It looks like a killer chicken."

"I tell you one thing they got right," said Jamal. "Raptors like to hunt in pairs."

Despite the urgency, Mr Pertwee smiled. "Very good, Jamal. Give yourself a gold star."

"Cool!" said Jamal with a grin, turning to make for the 'Superstars' chart on the wall.

"Not right now, Jamal!"

Jamal stopped amid the classroom chaos.

"Oh, yeah. Right."

Mr Pertwee sighed. "You are correct,

however. They do hunt in pairs. We're very

lucky we don't have a second raptor in here with us."

"Unless you count that one over there," said Jamal, pointing to the teacher's desk.

Everyone turned. There, dashing out from behind Mr Pertwee's briefcase, was a second velociraptor — slightly bigger and, if possible, angrier than the first.

Lizzy wailed again, this time joined by at least half a dozen of her classmates.

"Packed lunch!" exclaimed Sarah suddenly. "Who can get to their packed lunch?"

Jamal stared at his friend in surprise. "How can you be hungry at a time like this?"

"No!" said Sarah. "It's not for me. We can

use the food to lead the dinosaurs back to the time portal."

"That's a great idea!" said Mr Pertwee. He turned to address the class. "Who's near enough to their schoolbag that they can get their lunchbox out?"

"Me!" shouted Hussein from near the whiteboard. He produced his lunch and tossed it over to the teacher.

"Fab!" said Mr Pertwee, snatching the plastic box out of the air and opening it. "With any luck the raptors will like …" He sniffed one of Hussein's sandwiches. "What is this?"

"Beef paste, jam and pickle," replied Hussein. "It's an acquired taste."

"Let's just hope the dinosaurs acquire it quickly," said Mr Pertwee, tearing the sandwiches apart and making a trail back towards the time portal.

Luckily, they did. The newly arrived larger velociraptor especially enjoyed the sandwich. It lunged for the tasty treats, gobbling them down and easily being led towards its jungle home, where it disappeared back into the dense undergrowth.

That just left the smaller, more cautious of the two creatures. It sniffed at each bit of dropped sandwich, getting closer and closer to the exit, where it stopped to finally taste one of the hunks of bread and paste.

It was this EXACT moment when the huge head of a Tyrannosaurus Rex plunged through the time portal, and swallowed the velociraptor in one gulp.

CHAPTER FIVE
TROPHY

ROAR!

The T-Rex let out its angry cry and stomped into the classroom, crushing chairs, desks and the bowl of battery-powered sprouts under its massive feet.

The pupils screamed and ran for their lives.

The classroom door slammed open and Miss Howkins strode in. "PLEASE WILL YOU KEEP THE NOISE DOWN!" she bellowed.

"I'm trying to—" She stopped, glanced up at the huge dinosaur, down at the shuddering students, then back up to the T-Rex again.

"Never mind," she spluttered, spinning out of the room and slamming the door behind her.

Alice reached for the handle and tugged

it hard. But the door didn't move.

"I think … I think Miss Howkins has locked us in," she said.

"Don't be silly," said Mr Pertwee, one eye on the T-Rex as it devoured his briefcase. "Hussein, open the door, please."

Nodding, Hussein pulled at the door. It still didn't move.

"Alice is right, sir," he said. "It's locked."

"What?"

The teacher raced to join them and tried the door himself.

"Oh, dear. We do seem to be trapped."

The children's screams rose to fever pitch, causing the Tyrannosaurus to lift its head and let loose another fearsome bellow.

ROAR!

The children all rushed to the door at once, hammering on the wooden panels and shouting for help.

STOMP! STOMP! STOMP! STOMP!

They turned to see the vast dinosaur plodding towards them.

This is it, thought Sarah. This is how it will all end. We'll be squashed and eaten — and all before break time.

SQUEAK!

Everyone in the room froze — including the dinosaur.

SQUEAK! SQUEAK!

"Franklin!" cried Jamal. "You're back!"

The T-Rex looked down at the tiny

hamster sitting at its feet. Then, with a final cry —

RRROOOAAARRR!

— it ran back through the time portal and deep into the pre-historic forest beyond.

"Now!" yelled Mr Pertwee.

Sarah didn't need telling twice. She leapt for the portal, and grabbed the invisible thread. Pulling her hands apart, she tore it into pieces, completely destroying the doorway to the past.

Finally, the room fell silent. All that could be heard was the gentle sobbing of Lizzy, the faint buzz of several flattened sprouts, and Jamal making the kissy-kissy noise as he scooped Franklin up into his hands.

"How did that work?" asked Claire.

"Yeah," said Dan. "Why was a massive T-Rex scared of a tiny little hamster?"

Mr Pertwee shrugged. "There were mammals around at the time of the dinosaurs, but nothing exactly like Franklin, I suppose. And if a small mouse can terrify a huge elephant ..."

Jamal lowered his pet gently into his box and slotted the lid into place. "I'll take him home in my Hamster Transportation Unit and give him a big piece of carrot for saving us all!"

The whole class cheered loudly.

And Miss Howkins didn't say a word.

But, she did sneak back out of her

classroom and unlock the door to Class 4 when no-one was looking.

BRRRRRIIIIIINNNNGGG!

"OK, there's the bell!" shouted Mr Pertwee. He looked over to see Lizzy trying the door again and finding that it now opened.

"Go outside and get some fresh air. We have a LOT of clearing up to do after break time."

"Wait a minute!" cried Hussein. "What about The Big Boffin award?"

"Oh, yeah!" said Polly. "Who won?"

Mr Pertwee found the trophy lying on top of a coat, on the floor behind his desk. It wasn't too damaged, although the golden

brain wobbled about at the end of

its stick a bit.

"This prize was created for the pupil

whose scientific invention would do incredible things for the world," he said. "And I think we all know who deserves it the most, don't we, Sarah?"

Sarah beamed and took the trophy. "We do indeed, sir," she said. "The winner of the Sladen School Science Show is … Jamal Jones!"

"What?" exclaimed Jamal, genuinely surprised. "Really?"

Mr Pertwee nodded, "Really. Some of the inventions here may have had more scientific merit, but only one of them brought Franklin into school so that he could save us all."

With that, the pupils of Class 4 lifted

Jamal onto their shoulders, and marched out off towards the playground."

"Jamal! Jamal! Jamal!"

Jamal beamed happily. "Cool!"

After a moment, only Sarah and Mr Pertwee were left behind.

"I have to destroy my sewing needle, don't I?" she said.

Mr Pertwee nodded, "I'm afraid so. Why don't I go and see what Mr Honey has in his caretaker's storeroom that will help us?"

Sarah passed her sewing needle to Mr Pertwee. Then, with a final glance back at the destruction, Mr Pertwee left the room.

All was silent for a moment, until a tiny cry echoed out.

MRAWWW!

Something moved under a coat on

the back of a chair. A little lump shifted

awkwardly beneath the material, then a tiny baby T-Rex toddled into view.

"Mr Pertwee!" Sarah yelled, running after her teacher ...